Skin Like Mine

By Tiffany Elle Burgess

Illustrated by Takeia Marie

Gabrielle & Caleb,
Remember you are fearfully &
wonderfully made! Enjoy the
book!

Goode Stuff Publishing

Tiffany Elle Burgess

www.tiffanyelleburgess.com

To all of the beautiful women in my family, especially my Mom and 3 wonderful nieces. Rest in peace, Grandma, Aunt Lynda, and Aunt Alice.

I love you all to pieces.

-Tiffany Elle Burgess

♡ *There's a gymnast living inside my stomach!* ♡

Tabitha the Teenaged Tap-Dancing Dinosaur backpack? Check. Denim skirt? Check. White t-shirt? Check. Lucky red hair bows? Check. Hmmm, what am I missing? Brittany lay in bed wide awake, crossing things off her list while anxiously waiting for her mom to tell her it was time to get ready for school.

"Brit Bear, wake up, honey, and get dressed for school!" said Brittany's mother, yelling from her bedroom. Brittany jumped out of bed full of excitement. She quickly took her bath, brushed her teeth, and put on her clothes. She asked her parents if she could sleep in her school clothes the night before but the answer was a resounding, "no!" She ran to her parents' bathroom so her mother could brush her hair.

"Two puffs or one, Honey?" Brittany's mother asked.

"Mooooom," Brittany groaned. "Two, of course!" she said, smiling at her mother.

Two curly puffs were Brittany's signature hairstyle. She often wore her hair in two puffs with a bow at the top of each one. Brittany grabbed her backpack and ran downstairs to the kitchen.

"Good morning!" she said to her father and two older brothers as she sat down to eat her breakfast.

"Excited, Honey?" Brittany's father asked.

"Obviously!" said her older brother, Byron.

"Yes, Dad," she said while ignoring her brother's snide comment. "I'm so excited I can hardly eat. I can't wait to make new friends!" she exclaimed.

"Well, I know that won't be a problem for you, Brit Bear," her father assured, "but I think you may have forgotten something," he said, looking down at Brittany's bare feet.

"Oops, I forgot my shoes!" said Brittany, cupping her hand over her mouth and giggling at her father's observation.

She quickly ran back upstairs, nearly knocking her mother down on the way up.

"Sorry, Mom!" she yelled.

She threw on her favorite red shoes to match her lucky hair bows and took a deep breath. *Now* she was officially ready for school. Brittany wanted to look perfect because today was no ordinary school day. No, today was Brittany's first day at her new school, Northern Heights Middle School.

Brittany Baker is a happy-go-lucky 10-year-old girl who loves to tap dance. She has a style of her own—from head to toe—and a smile as bright as the sun and as wide as an ocean. She recently moved to Atlanta, Georgia with her mother, Jean, a professor at a local college, her father, Carl, Sr., an engineer, and her two older brothers, Carl, Jr. (affectionately called CJ), and Byron.

Brittany loves her father dearly but she has a very special bond with her mother, Jean. Their bond is one that cannot be described with words. She misses her friends at her old school in Illinois but making friends has never been a problem for Brittany so she is quite eager to meet her new classmates at Northern Heights.

The closer they got to her new school, the more nervous Brittany became. By the time they pulled up to Northern Heights, Brittany's stomach was doing so many backflips she felt like a gymnast was living inside of it! She kissed her mother goodbye, grabbed her

things, and hopped out of the car to meet her new homeroom teacher who was waiting for her on the front steps of the school.

"Good morning, Brittany. Welcome to Northern Heights Middle School," greeted Ms. Allen.

Brittany turned around to wave goodbye to her mother one last time before heading into her new school.

As she walked through the big red doors of the school, she thought to herself, red is my favorite color, this is definitely a good sign. Brittany's eyes grew bigger and bigger as she and Ms. Allen walked to her classroom. The building was much larger than her old school in Illinois and there were a lot more students walking the halls.

Her stomach was no longer doing backflips. Instead, it was doing full somersaults!

3

She spent most of the day learning where everything was in her new school. Although she met a number of children during her classes and lunch time, she hadn't quite made any new friends.

At the end of the school day she asked Ms. Allen to walk her to Peachy Keen, Northern Height's after school program. Because school ended before her parents could leave work, Brittany would be spending at least an hour in the program every day until her mother came to get her. This didn't bother Brittany at all. Her parents told her that several children at Northern Heights attended Peachy Keen so she figured the after school program would be the perfect place to make new friends.

♡ *Welcome to Peachy Keen!* ♡

When she walked into Peachy Keen, she noticed there were a lot of children just as her parents had stated, and they were all doing different things. Some of the children were doing their homework, some were playing games on the computer (such as checkers and chess), one little girl had her head buried deep in a book, and a few of the other children were sitting in a circle talking to each other. Noticing that Brittany did not know where to sit, Ms. Allen smiled, put her hand on Brittany's shoulder and said,

"Brittany, I have an idea. Come with me."

Ms. Allen walked Brittany over to the circle where some of the children were talking and laughing.

"Children, I want you all to meet someone. This is Brittany Baker," said Ms. Allen. "She is a new fifth grader here at Northern Heights. Please make her feel welcomed," she continued.

"Yes, Ms. Allen," replied the children in unison.

Brittany sat down in the circle and began to introduce herself.

"Hi, I'm Brittany. My friends call me Brit," she said flashing her bright, wide smile and waving her hand at the other children.

"Hi, Brittany," said the two girls at the same time.

They were twins. Brittany noticed they were dressed alike from head to toe and wore the same hairstyle, very long ponytails, with shiny yellow headbands.

"I'm Kayla," said one of the twins.

"And I'm Hayley," the other quickly chimed in.

They even sounded alike to Brittany.

"This is Tyler," Kayla said pointing to the boy sitting next to her, "and that's Juan," she said, pointing to the other boy sitting in the circle.

"Where are you from?" Kayla asked.

"Illinois. My dad got a new job so we moved here to Atlanta," explained Brittany.

"Well, we know everyone at Northern Heights," boasted Hayley, "so if you have any questions about anything, you should ask us," she continued.

"Yeah, Hayley and Kayla are the prettiest, most popular girls in school," said Tyler as the girls began to blush.

"Welcome to Northern Heights and Peachy Keen, Brittany," said **Juan.**

And indeed Brittany did feel welcomed. Everyone had been so nice to her thus far. Ms. Allen was great and her first day of classes had been easy breezy. Overall, Brittany considered the first day at her new school a big success.

The children continued to talk about their favorite songs and the last movies they had seen. Brittany was beginning to think she had officially made her first, new friends at Northern Heights, which made her feel very happy and relieved. She was in the middle of telling the other children about her last tap-dance recital back in Illinois when she heard her mother's voice.

"Uh oh, that's my mom. I have to go," said Brittany to the children whom she considered her newfound friends.

"Where's your mom?" asked Kayla, looking around the room.

"Right there," said Brittany, pointing to her mother who was standing at the door talking to Ms. Allen.

"Really?" asked Hayley with a surprised look on her face. She whispered something to Kayla and they both began to snicker. Kayla then whispered something to Tyler and Juan and soon all four children were laughing!

"What?" asked Brittany, confused by the other children's laughter.

No one replied.

"What's so funny?" she asked again, growing annoyed by their snickering.

"Nothing, it's just, well—," began Kayla.

"You don't really look like your mom," interrupted Hayley, still giggling.

Confused by what Hayley said, Brittany looked over at her mother who was engrossed in conversation with Ms. Allen, and replied,

"Yes, I do!"

"Uh, no, you don't," the twins quickly rebutted.

"No one has ever told you that?" asked Kayla.

"Maybe she's adopted," teased Juan.

"I am not adopted!" said Brittany sternly. "Why would you say that?" she asked angrily.

"I mean, she's, um, a lot lighter than you and her hair is long, too, kind of like ours," said Hayley, stroking her ponytail. "Your mom is really pretty. You just don't look like her, that's all," she continued.

The children continued to snicker and before Brittany could respond to Hayley's comments, her mother called her name to go home. She hastily grabbed her backpack and headed towards the door. She looked back at the twins and the boys who were still laughing at her expense. Brittany didn't understand. What were they talking about? Of course she looked like her mother. No one had ever mentioned that she didn't look like her mother before, at least not to her face, so this was certainly news to her.

During the car ride home Brittany thought about what the twins and Juan had said to her at Peachy Keen. She looked at her mother's hair and skin through the rearview mirror. Her mother, noticing that Brittany was quietly staring at her, began to make funny faces at her to break the silence, and soon Brittany began to laugh.

"You're so silly, Mom," she said. "I'm silly, just like you, right?" Brittany asked.

"Of course you are, you're my little Brit Bear!" her mother replied.

When they got home, Brittany went straight upstairs to her room. She threw her backpack on the floor and sat on her bed with her hands rested underneath her chin. Although her mother's affirmation that she was silly just like her was nice, it wasn't quite enough to erase the children's words and laughter from her mind. She began to wonder if they were right. She hadn't really thought about it before but her mother's skin was lighter than hers and well, her hair was much longer. If her mother was pretty and she didn't look like her, did that mean she wasn't pretty? The more Brittany mulled it over, the more concerned she grew.

"Brit Bear, wash your hands and get ready for dinner," yelled her mother from the kitchen.

Brittany washed her hands and ran downstairs. As she sat at the dinner table beside her brother, Byron, she couldn't help but stare across the table at her mother, Jean. Brittany began to look down at her arms; they looked like milk chocolate. Her mother's arms didn't look like chocolate. Brittany's eyes were dark brown; whereas, her mother's eyes were a lighter brown. Her mother had long, straight hair but Brittany's hair was curly. Brittany continued to compare herself to her mother when her father called her name.

"Brit Bear," said her father.

Brittany didn't answer.

"Brittany!" he repeated.

"Yes, Dad?" she said somewhat startled as she didn't hear him call her name the first time.

"How was school, Honey?" he asked.

"Um, fine," she mumbled.

Her father and brothers couldn't help but notice that her answer lacked the same enthusiasm she spoke with earlier that morning.

"Tired?" asked her brother, Byron. "Fifth grade can be so exhausting, huh?" he said mockingly.

Brittany was too preoccupied watching her mother's every move to respond to Byron with something equally as sarcastic. She decided she had to prove the other children wrong. From now on, she would do everything just like her mother. At dinner she paid very close attention to everything her mother did. She laughed when her mother laughed. When her mother took a sip of water, she took a sip of water. She even tried to chew her food just like her mother.

Later on that evening, as Brittany lay in the bed thinking about the next day of school, her parents came into her room to say good night.

"Good night, Brit Bear," said her parents as they each took turns kissing her forehead.

"Did you say your prayers?" asked her mother.

"Oh, I forgot," said Brittany.

"Well, hurry up and say your prayers. It's past your bedtime and you have to get up early for school in the morning," urged her mother as her parents turned off her light and cracked the door to her bedroom.

Brittany waited until she heard her parents' bedroom door close and then climbed out of bed. She kneeled down beside her bed and clasped her hands tightly together. She began to say her prayers like she always did, except this prayer was different from any other prayer she had ever said.

"Dear God," she began. "Um, thank you for a good day at my new school but," she paused, "could you please prove the kids at Peachy Keen wrong and make me look more like my mom?" she asked. "I want to be pretty just like her. Amen," said Brittany as she climbed back into her bed.

Tomorrow morning, she thought, I'll look more like my mom and I'll show those twins, Tyler, and Juan just how wrong they are.

♡ *Introducing: "Operation No Peachy Keen!"* ♡

The next morning, Brittany sprang out of bed to see if she looked any different. She ran to the bathroom that she and her brothers shared but much to her chagrin, the door was closed and locked.

"CJ, Byron!!!" she screamed. "Whoever is in there, please hurry up!" she yelled as she banged on the door.

"Calm down!" her brother, CJ, replied from inside the bathroom. "I'll be out in a minute!"
Brittany, becoming more anxious, continued to bang on the bathroom door.

"Ceeeeee Jaaaaaay!" she screamed.

"Brittany!" her father interrupted. "Stop that yelling this early in the morning. You can use our bathroom," he said, pointing to his and her mother's bedroom.

"Ugh!" Brittany grumbled.
While walking towards her parents' bedroom, the bathroom door abruptly flew open and CJ walked out.

"It's all yours, Brit," said CJ, annoyed by what he considered his little sister's early morning temper tantrum.
Brittany quickly turned around and ran into the bathroom, closing and locking the door behind her.

"Finally," she sighed.
She slowly approached the mirror with her hands over her eyes. When she removed them, she took a long hard look at her eyes first. Hmph, she thought to herself. They didn't look any different. She still had the same big, pretty, piercing, brown eyes. Then she carefully examined her skin. No change there either.

In fact, nothing had changed! She still had the same dark skin that resembled milk chocolate and curly, dark brown hair. Brittany was disappointed that she didn't look more like her mother. She began to pout until it dawned on her there was one thing she could indeed change herself.

After she got dressed for school, she stood at the top of the staircase and carefully listened to make sure her parents and brothers were in the kitchen. Once she was certain that everyone was downstairs eating breakfast, she quietly tiptoed into her parents' bathroom, plugged in her mother's hair straightener, and began to brush her hair. Just as she started to clamp the hot straightening iron down on her beautiful, curly hair, her mother walked in.

"Brittany Alexis Baker!" her mother shouted. "What in the world do you think you are doing?" she asked.

Stunned, Brittany dropped the hot straightening iron and attempted to explain.

"I, I just wanted to wear my hair like yours, Mom," she began.

"Since when do you want your hair straightened?" her mother asked. "And you know better than to touch my hair straightener. You could have burned yourself!" her mother scolded as she grabbed the brush and proceeded to put Brittany's hair in her signature style.

"Now, two puffs or one?" she angrily asked Brittany.

"No puffs," muttered Brittany under her breath.

Her mother put her hair in two puffs with a bow at the top of each one and ordered her to go downstairs to eat breakfast.

"We'll talk about this later, Miss Brittany," her mother said.

Any time her mother addressed her as "Miss Brittany", she knew she was in big trouble! Brittany sluggishly walked downstairs to the kitchen. She was not looking forward to going to school, more importantly, she dreaded seeing the twins, Juan, and Tyler at the after school program. As she sat at the kitchen table playing with her cereal she decided if she could somehow avoid Peachy Keen for the rest of the week, she would be just fine. She resolved that God needed a *little* more time to answer her prayer. Brittany was a clever little girl so she devised "Operation No Peachy Keen" to give God just that, more time.

Later on that day, Brittany delayed going to Peachy Keen as long as she could. She figured she only needed to make it through one more day at the after school program and then she could put "Operation No Peachy Keen" into effect. For most of the hour, she helped Ms. Allen clean her classroom and organize the computer lab for the next day. By the time she got to Peachy Keen, much to her delight, the twins, Tyler, and Juan had gone home.

15

Over the next few days, Brittany went to great lengths to avoid attending the after school program altogether. On Wednesday, her mother surprisingly received a phone call at work from Ms. Allen stating that Brittany was not feeling well. Ms. Allen informed Mrs. Baker that Brittany's stomach began to hurt during the last class period of the day and perhaps she or her husband should come and get her as soon as school ended. As a result, Brittany's father left work early to pick her up. Ironically, as soon as she got home, Brittany miraculously felt well enough to eat all of her dinner, share a big bowl of vanilla ice cream with her brother, Byron, for dessert, and ask if she could attend her tap-dancing class. This did not go unnoticed by her parents but they figured the food she ate for lunch upset her stomach and allowed her to attend tap-dancing class later on that evening after all.

♡ *Day 1 down, a few more to go!* ♡

On Thursday morning, Brittany lay in her bed devising yet another scheme to get out of going to the after school program. She knew she couldn't say that she was sick, so she needed another excuse to skip the program. She decided she would ask her father to pick her up as soon as school ended and take her back to work with him. That morning at breakfast she put Day 2 of "Operation No Peachy Keen" into action.

"Daddy," she began, innocently smiling at him, "can you come and get me from school and take me back to work with you?" she asked. "I have to write a report on what I want to be when I grow up and I think I want to be an engineer, just like you," she said, batting her big, brown eyes at her father.

Flattered and beyond excited to hear that his daughter wanted to follow in his footsteps, Brittany's father happily agreed.

"Oh how nice, Brit Bear!" he said. "It is last minute but I think I can slip away from the office quickly to come and get you."

"Wait a minute!" interrupted Byron. "I thought you wanted to be a professor like mom or open a tap-dance school or something," he continued with a look of utter disbelief on his face. "Besides, I've been to dad's job, Brit, and boy is it booooor—" began Byron before he abruptly stopped himself from finishing the word, boring.

"Byron Baker, be supportive," said their father who was annoyed by Byron's claim that his job was boring.

"Yeah, Byron, be supportive!" repeated Brittany, as she breathed a sigh of relief.

Whew! That was a close call, she thought. After all, Byron was right.

She didn't want to be an engineer like her father and she felt guilty for lying to him but she absolutely, positively could not go back to the after school program. Not just yet. God needed more time to answer her prayer.

At the end of the school day, Brittany's father was outside waiting for her. She went to his job and spent an hour learning about mechanical engineering. Although she enjoyed spending time with her father, the visit to his job confirmed for Brittany that she definitely did not want to be an engineer when she grew up.

"I can't wait to read your report!" said her father excitedly as they walked into the house.

"My report?" asked Brittany.

It had completely slipped her mind that she told her father she had to write a report on what she wanted to be when she grew up to get him to pick her up from school in the first place.

"Oh, yeah, my report. Me either, Dad," Brittany murmured as she walked upstairs to her bedroom.

She was in no mood to write a "fake" report but she knew she had to write something in order to keep up her lie.

"Maybe I didn't think this plan through very well," she whispered to herself as she sat down at her desk and began to write.

♡ *Two days down, one more to go!* ♡

On Friday morning, Brittany woke up relieved that she had made it to the end of the school week and "Operation No Peachy Keen" had been such a success. She began to celebrate as she got dressed for school, until she suddenly realized she was fresh out of creative ways to avoid Peachy Keen later on that afternoon. She definitely was not ready to go back. After all, God still hadn't answered her prayer!

Brittany spent the entire school day trying to figure out how she could skip Peachy Keen. She thought long and hard but she just couldn't seem to come up with anything, and before she knew it the school day had ended. When Ms. Allen briefly stepped out of the classroom to talk to Principal Johnson, a panicked Brittany pretended to walk towards Peachy Keen with the other children in the program, and then snuck into the girls' bathroom when no one was looking. She thought she could wait there until it was time for her mother to pick her up from school. She grabbed some paper towels and went into the last stall. She carefully laid the paper towels across the lid of the toilet and sat down. As she was sitting there, twiddling her thumbs and patiently waiting for the time to pass, she heard the bathroom door spring open.

"Brittany Baker?"

It was Ms. Johnson, Northern Heights Middle School's Head Principal!

"Are you in here?" asked Ms. Johnson.

Brittany sat as quiet as a mouse, trying to hold her breath until Ms. Johnson left. Her cheeks were so full of air they looked like she had a balloon in each one.

Her plan would have worked, too, except Ms. Johnson didn't leave.

Instead, much to Brittany's dismay, Ms. Johnson began to open each one of the bathroom stall doors. When she got to the last stall where Brittany was hiding, it was locked.

"Brittany?" Ms. Johnson called again.

Brittany's stomach began to do somersaults again. She knew this feeling all too well and before she could stop herself, she let out a huge sigh. Her cheeks deflated like someone had popped them with a sharp pin, and of course Ms. Johnson heard it.

"Brittany Baker, open this door right now!" ordered Ms. Johnson.

Realizing that she was caught, Brittany reluctantly climbed off the toilet and unlocked the door. There Ms. Johnson stood with her hands on her hips and a grimace on her face. Brittany knew she had a lot of explaining to do.

Brittany sat quietly in the chair outside of the Principal's office while her mother spoke to Ms. Johnson. She desperately wanted to hear what they were saying but realized she was in enough trouble and better sit there and "not move a muscle" as her mother instructed.

"Thank you, Ms. Johnson," Brittany heard her mother say as the door opened.

"You are welcome, Mrs. Baker," Ms. Johnson said. "Brittany," she began with a smile on her face, "I will see you on Monday."

"Yes, ma'am," Brittany replied.

Since Ms. Johnson was smiling at her, Brittany started to think she might not be in *too* much trouble. Boy was she mistaken. As soon as they got in the car, Brittany's mother began expressing just how disappointed she was in her behavior and it continued the entire way home. Brittany wanted to tell her mother what the other children had said to her and how they had laughed at her earlier that week, but she didn't know how. Besides, soon God would answer her prayer and her problem would be solved anyway. So, she decided to sit there silently and take her mother's admonishment, and an admonishment it was!

When they got home, Brittany's parents told her to wash her hands and get ready for dinner but she could not have any ice cream for dessert or participate in "Movie Night". Friday nights were "Movie Night" in the Baker household. Every Friday night she and her brothers took turns choosing a movie. They usually ordered a pizza, and as a treat their mother allowed them to eat in the living room while watching the movie instead of the dining room. Brittany loved "Movie Night." She looked forward to it every week. She had not seen her mother this upset with her since she and her brother, Byron, broke her favorite lamp while playing basketball in the house.

She knew she had better take her bath, think about her actions, and go to bed just as her parents ordered.

As her family watched a movie downstairs, Brittany lay in bed, teary-eyed, thinking about her first week at Northern Heights. She couldn't believe how horribly it had gone. She had gotten into so much trouble for trying to skip the after school program and she felt bad for the lies she had told to her parents. She hoped by the next day her prayer would be answered and she could put an end to "Operation No Peachy Keen" for good.

♡ *My prayer has finally been answered...or has it?* ♡

The next morning, Brittany woke up and ran straight to the bathroom. Surely she had given God enough time to answer her prayer. On the way to the bathroom, she overheard her parents talking in their bedroom.

"I just don't know what has gotten into her, Carl, she has been acting differently this entire week," said Brittany's mother.

"I think she's just having a hard time adjusting to her new school, Jean. She'll be fine," her father replied.

"Hmmm, I guess," her mother sighed. "I am going to have a talk with her anyway," she continued.

Brittany quickly closed the bathroom door. She turned on the light, stood in front of the mirror, closed her eyes, and quickly opened them, hoping to see something different staring back at her. Again, nothing had changed. She had the same skin, eyes, and hair. Brittany was devastated. Nothing had gone as planned this week. She hadn't made any new friends at school, she lied to her parents, disappointed Ms. Allen and Ms. Johnson, missed "Movie Night" with her family, spent the entire week avoiding the after school program, and she *still* didn't look more like her mother. Overwhelmed, Brittany began to cry.

When she came out of the bathroom and walked back into her bedroom, her mother was sitting on her bed waiting for her.

"There you are, Brittany," she said.

She looked at Brittany who was sniffling and trying to hide her tears.

"Oh, Brit Bear, come here," her mother said.

"You aren't in *that* much trouble. Sit down and talk to me," said Brittany's mother as she patted the bed and motioned for Brittany to take a seat beside her.

23

Brittany didn't know where to begin. She was so upset. Before she knew it, she blurted out,

"Am I adopted, Mom?"

"What are you talking about?" asked her mother, shocked by the question. "Of course not, Brittany," she declared.

"Well," Brittany began, "I, I....," she stuttered.

"Brit Bear, you know you can always talk to me," said her mother, drying Brittany's eyes.

Brittany knew she had no choice but to tell her mother the truth, so she decided to start from the very beginning.

"Well, I was having a good first day of school until I went to Peachy Keen. That's where I met the twins, Tyler, and Juan."

"The twins, Tyler, and Juan? Who are they?" Brittany's mother probed further.

"Yes, I met the twins, Hayley and Kayla, and the boys, Tyler and Juan, my first day at Peachy Keen. The twins are the prettiest, most popular girls at Northern Heights and I thought I had made four new friends," said Brittany. "Well, until you came to get me," she continued.

"And then what happened?" her mother asked intently listening to Brittany's story.

Brittany lowered her head and replied,

"Well, the twins said I didn't look like you because your skin is lighter than mine and your hair is straight and long. And then Juan said maybe I was adopted. They were all laughing about it. So I prayed to God that he would make me look more like you. I mean, I want to be pretty like you, Mom. I'm sorry I didn't tell you everything sooner," whimpered Brittany.

Brittany's mother lifted her head and looked her in the eyes.

"Brittany Alexis Baker, you are the smartest, most beautiful little girl I know," began her mother.

"But why don't I look like you? I mean, Hayley and Kayla are Black, too, and they look more like you than I do. Why?" interrupted Brittany, yearning for an explanation. Her mother, who was saddened by what her daughter had experienced at the after school program, took a deep breath and asked,

"Do you know who you really look like, Brit Bear?"

"No, ma'am," answered Brittany.

"Well, first of all, our family, like a lot of Black families, is very diverse, Honey," her mother began. "And the differences in our skin tones and physical features should be celebrated, not used to separate us. You, Brit Bear, get your beautiful skin tone from your dad."

"My skin tone?" asked Brittany.

"Yes, the color of your skin," said her mother. "Those big, pretty, dark brown eyes of yours are from your grandfather, my dad. Your curly hair, well that is from me. I just straighten mine, you know that," said Brittany's mother. "You see, you are a wonderful combination of so many people in your family, people who love you so very much," her mother continued. "And that gorgeous, bright, wide smile of yours, do you know who you got that from?" her mother asked.

"Grandmom?" Brittany guessed as she shrugged her shoulders unsure from whom she got her smile.

"No one. That is uniquely yours," said Brittany's mother with a big smile on her face.

"Brit Bear, you are growing up," her mother said. "And as you get older you will meet a lot of different people. Some people will say things to hurt your feelings, some on purpose and some on an accident. Some will look like you. Some won't. But it is not what people say to you that counts, it is how you respond," continued her mother. "What you have to remember is that beauty comes in all different shades, shapes, and sizes. It cannot be defined by what you see on television or in magazines, nor can it be defined by what others say to or about you. You have to be confident in who you are, Brittany Baker, and you must define beauty for yourself," said Brittany's mother as she pointed her finger at her.

26

"Do you understand what I am saying?" her mother asked.

"Yes, I understand, Mom," said Brittany. "Mom," continued Brittany curious about one more thing, "why is it so important how I look anyway?"

"Oh, Brit Bear," her mother began, "it really isn't that important." "At the end of the day, it's your inside, how you behave and treat others, that counts the most," she said while placing her hand on Brittany's heart.

Her mother told her to take a bath and get dressed as they were going to have a special "Girls Day Out", just the two of them. Before she headed out of Brittany's room, she asked her one last question,

"Do you know why God did not answer your prayer? Why he didn't change you to look more like me?"

Brittany shook her head "no."

"Because you are already perfect in God's eyes," said her mother as she winked her eye at Brittany.

"I love you, Mom," Brittany replied with a big smile on her face.

"I love you, too, Brit Bear," said Brittany's mother.

Brittany felt so much better after talking to her mother. It was like a huge weight had been lifted from her shoulders. She wished she would have told her mother everything sooner. She learned three big lessons that morning—it is always better to be honest with her parents when something bothers her instead of keeping it to herself, true beauty comes from within, and most importantly, she is perfectly made by God.

The Bakers went on to have a wonderful weekend. Brittany played video games with her brothers. She went shopping for new clothes and got a manicure with her mother.

She ate ice cream with her father and practiced for her next tap-dancing recital. Overall, it was the perfect end to a crazy week.

♡ *Day 1 of "Operation Yes to Peachy Keen!"* ♡

By Monday morning, Brittany was prepared to go back to Northern Heights and Peachy Keen. She leapt out of bed, put on her clothes, and grabbed her Tabitha the Teenaged Tap-Dancing Dinosaur backpack. As usual, she ran down to her parents' bathroom so her mother could brush her hair. Brittany's mother, who decided to wear her hair in a curly ponytail to work instead of straightening it, began to fix her hair.

"Two puffs or one?" Brittany's mother asked.

"Mooom," Brittany bemoaned. "Don't be silly, two of course," she said, grinning at her mother in the mirror.

"That's my girl!" her mother exclaimed.

As they got closer to the school, Brittany began to experience that very familiar flip flopping feeling in the pit of her stomach. Although she felt much better after the conversation she had with her mother a couple of days ago, she realized she was still a little nervous about seeing the twins, Juan, and Tyler at Peachy Keen later on that afternoon. As she got out of the car, her mother rolled down the window and said,

"Remember to be confident. You were perfectly made by God! Have a good day, Brit Bear!"

"Thanks, Mom," she said as she headed towards the big red doors of the school.

Fortunately for Brittany, her school day went very well. Her classes were still easy breezy. Ms. Johnson smiled at her in the hallway on the way to lunch, and Ms. Allen accepted her apology for her behavior the previous week. She also reassured Brittany that she could always come to her if she needed anything. By the end of the day, Brittany's stomach was strangely calm and she realized she wasn't as worried about going to the after school program anymore.

After the school bell rang, Ms. Allen took Brittany aside and asked,

"Do you want me to walk you to Peachy Keen?"

Brittany smiled and replied, "No, ma'am. I think I know where it is."

As Brittany walked into the after school program, she saw some children doing their homework, some children playing games (this time Monopoly and Go Fish), the same little girl with her head buried deep in yet another book, and of course, the twins, Hayley and Kayla, sitting in a circle talking to none other than Tyler and Juan.

"Hi, Brittany," said Kayla, snickering and waving for Brittany to come over to the circle.

Brittany thought about her mother's words and walked over to the circle where the twins, Tyler, and Juan were sitting with her head held high.

"Where have you been?" asked Hayley as the other children giggled.

"Is your mom coming today?" asked Tyler slyly.

"If that's really her mom," whispered Kayla, still giggling.

"Yes, she is," said Brittany with her arms folded.

All four children continued to laugh when Brittany abruptly interrupted them.

"You know what," she began, "beauty comes in all different shades, shapes, and sizes, but at the end of the day it doesn't even matter what you look like. It's not the outside that counts anyway, it's the inside," she continued while pointing to her heart. " So, my mom may not have skin like mine, but she is still my mom and she loves me very much!" Brittany asserted.

31

The twins, Tyler, and Juan sat quietly, shocked by Brittany's courage. They couldn't believe she had stood up to them. Before Brittany turned around to walk away, she looked all four children in the eyes and said,

"And just so you know, I wouldn't change a thing about myself. Do you know why?" she asked.

"Why?" asked Tyler still in awe of Brittany's confidence.

"Because God already made me perfect just the way I am!" she exclaimed.

Brittany was so proud of herself. It felt amazing to stand up to the twins, Juan, and Tyler. She sat down at one of the tables by herself and began to take her homework out of her backpack when she suddenly heard Ms. Allen call the other children's names.

"Kayla, Hayley, Tyler, and Juan, please come with me," said Ms. Allen who, unbeknownst to Brittany, had been listening the entire time.

She heard everything! The four children slowly got up with fear in their eyes because they knew they were in trouble. They hesitantly followed Ms. Allen into the hallway as Brittany watched with a smirk on her face. She began to do her Math homework when the little girl who always had her head buried deep in a book came over and sat down beside her.

"Hi there, I'm Diya," said the little girl.

"Hi, Diya, I'm Brittany, but my friends call me Brit," said Brittany.

"Cute backpack. Do you like to tap dance?" asked Diya.

"Yes, I do!" responded Brittany enthusiastically.

"I dance, too!" exclaimed Diya. "Right now I am learning Kathak, a dance from my home country, India."

"Ka, Kathak?" repeated Brittany. "What's that?" she asked Diya.

"My teacher said it's a classical dance that was once used for ancient story telling or something like that. The moves are really cool. Watch, I'll show you," said Diya as she stood up and began to show Brittany some of the basic moves from the dance she had been learning. Brittany, who was beyond excited to learn a new dance, quickly got up and tried to mimic what Diya was doing.

The two girls spent the next hour getting to know each other. They laughed and danced. They talked about everything from their favorite songs to the last books they each had read. It turned out the girls had a great deal in common, much more than they even knew.

Brittany was in the middle of showing Diya the routine from her last recital when Diya said she had to leave.

"Aw, my parents are here. I'll see you tomorrow, Brit," said Diya, grabbing her things.

Brittany looked around the room but she didn't see anyone who remotely looked like Diya. She did, however, notice a man who reminded her a lot of her own father and a woman who was much, much lighter than her mother. Brittany was extremely surprised!

As Diya began to leave Peachy Keen with her parents, she looked back and smiled at Brittany.

"Hey, Brit," she called.

"Yeah, Diya?" replied Brittany.

"As you can see, my mom doesn't have skin like mine either,"
continued Diya, beaming from ear to ear.

Brittany smiled back at her and both girls began to laugh.

Shortly after Diya left, Brittany's mother walked into Peachy Keen.

"Hi, Honey," said her mother.

Brittany grabbed her backpack and ran to give her mother a hug. As
they walked out of the school, Brittany's mother took her by the hand
and asked,

"Did you have a good day, Brit Bear?"

"Yes, I did, and guess what, Mom. Guess what!" an excited
Brittany exclaimed.

"What?" Brittany's mother asked anxiously awaiting her news.

Brittany, with a smile as bright as the sun

and as wide as an ocean, replied,

"I finally made my first, new friend!"

~THE END~

76532362R00023

Made in the USA
Columbia, SC
05 September 2017

A Collection of Forehead-Slapping Fun

Paul Sloane & Des MacHale

PUZZLE
WRIGHT
PRESS

New York

PUZZLE
WRIGHT
PRESS
New York

An Imprint of Sterling Publishing
387 Park Avenue South
New York, NY 10016

© 2013 by Paul Sloane and Des MacHale
All images used under license from Shutterstock.com

ISBN 978-1-4027-9910-5

Distributed in Canada by Sterling Publishing
c⁄o Canadian Manda Group, 165 Dufferin Street
Toronto, Ontario, Canada M6K 3H6
Distributed in the United Kingdom by GMC Distribution Services
Castle Place, 166 High Street, Lewes, East Sussex, England BN7 1XU
Distributed in Australia by Capricorn Link (Australia) Pty. Ltd.
P.O. Box 704, Windsor, NSW 2756, Australia

For information about custom editions, special sales, and premium and
corporate purchases, please contact Sterling Special Sales at 800-805-5489
or specialsales@sterlingpublishing.com.

Manufactured in the United States of America

2   4   6   8   10   9   7   5   3   1

www.puzzlewright.com

Contents

Introduction
5

Puzzles
7

Answers
76

Introduction

In our series of lateral thinking puzzle books we often included sections of "Wally Tests"—mean, low, nasty, trick questions. (We don't have anything against people named "Wally"; it's a U.K. slang term. An American equivalent might be "Blockhead Test.") We expected them to be most popular with younger readers, but as it happens, all ages proved to enjoy them.

Everyone, it seems, like a good trick question—one that completely stumps you, yet the answer is obvious once you hear it. A really good one makes you want to kick yourself. So we put together a collection of our favorites, and here it is! Please do not write to complain that some of the answers are silly, unfair, or illogical; we plead guilty as charged on all counts. Just enjoy the puzzles even as you groan at the answers. Because then comes the real fun—inflicting them on your family and friends. (And a quick note about that: Some of these puzzles will work *better* when you try them on other people, because they hinge on tricks of pronunciation. All such "out loud" questions are presented in italics.)

Although these puzzles are just for entertainment, there is still a message behind the fun: We all make assumptions about things. Each of us is at times predictable, lazy, or routine in our thinking. These trick questions teach us to check our assumptions, to think differently, and to realize that we do not have all the answers—even to seemingly easy questions like these!

—Paul Sloane and Des MacHale

1. What can I put in my left hand that I cannot put in my right hand?

2. If two peacocks lay two eggs in two days, how many eggs can **one peacock** lay in four days?

3. How many cubic feet of earth are there in a hole measuring 3 feet wide by 4 feet long by 5 feet deep?

4. Why do Chinese men eat more **rice** than Japanese men?

5. In what sport do half of the contestants wear metal shoes?

6. What do you call people born in San Francisco?

7. Why could Al Capone never get out of prison?

8. Where does yesterday always come after today?

9. *What should you do if you go into town and see a spaceman?*

10. Do you know how long cars should be washed?

11. Where was Queen Cleopatra's temple?

12. My uncle's sister is not my aunt. How come?

13. What is yours but other people use it more than you?

14. Joan was born on Christmas Day but always celebrates her birthday in summer. Why?

15. Two girls were born on the same date in the same year and have the same father and the same mother, yet they are not twins. How come?

16. What two things that you can eat can you never have for

breakfast?

17. If a farmer raises wheat in dry weather, what does he raise in wet weather?

18. How many successful **parachute** jumps does a trainee parachutist in the U.S. army have to make before graduating from jump school?

19. How can you tell the score of any football game before it starts?

20. A horse is tied to a piece of rope ten yards long. There is a stack of hay thirty yards away from the horse. How does the horse eat the hay?

21. When does $11 + 2 = 1$?

22. Removing an appendix is called an appendectomy; removing tonsils is called a tonsillectomy. What is it called when they remove a growth from your head?

23. If you find a $100 bill on the ground, should you keep it?

24. Where do the biggest potatoes grow?

25. Rungs on a rope ladder attached to a boat are one foot apart. At low tide five rungs are above the water and the tide rises at one foot per hour. How many rungs are above the water after four hours?

26. How can you drop a raw egg onto a concrete floor without cracking it?

27. How do you make a Maltese cross with just one match without breaking it?

28. If you had three apples and four oranges in one hand and four apples and three oranges in the other hand, what would you have?

29. Is a **duel** a good way of finding out who is right?

30. In a standard game of draw poker, a royal flush is a better hand than **four aces,** and yet a player with four aces can never lose to a player with a royal flush. Why?

31. Which would you prefer: an old ten-dollar bill or a new one?

32. What invention, first discovered in ancient times, allows people to see through solid walls?

33. You have two **buckets** full of water, one at 20 degrees Fahrenheit and the other at 20 degrees Centigrade. You drop identical coins into each bucket. Which coin hits the base of its bucket first?

34. Which is correct to say: "The yolk of an egg is white" or "The yolk of an egg are white"?

35. A man carefully pointed his car due east and then drove for two miles. He was then two miles west of where he started from. How come?

36. What is it that after you take away the whole, some remains?

37. A man bought a **parrot** guaranteed to repeat every word it heard, but it never said anything. Why?

38. Where was the Declaration of Independence signed?

39. You have a log weighing exactly two pounds. You saw it into two pieces of the same weight. How much does each piece weigh?

40. A girl took her dog for a walk. The dog did not walk in front of her nor behind her, nor on one side of her. How come?

41. A girl claimed her father was older than her grandfather. Could she have been telling the truth?

42. If it takes five minutes to hard-boil an egg, how long does it take to hard-boil three eggs?

43. What can speak every language in the world?

44. A farmer has three black cows, four brown cows, and five white cows. How many cows can say they are the same color as another cow?

45. If the vice president of the United States were killed, who would then become president?

46. Which type of candle burns longer: beeswax or tallow?

47. A farmer had four haystacks in one field and twice as many in each of his other two fields. He put the haystacks from all three fields together. All together, how many haystacks did he now have?

48. What five letter word becomes shorter when you add two letters to it?

49. What has four legs and only one foot?

50. When a man drives to work wearing an overcoat it takes him an hour and twenty minutes. When he drives to work not wearing an overcoat it takes him only eighty minutes. Why?

51. Why did **Beethoven** never finish the Unfinished Symphony?

52. What common word is pronounced wrongly by over half of all Yale and Harvard graduates?

53. What gets larger the more you take away?

54. What was the U.S. president's name in 1900?

55. Rearrange these letters to make one word: **NEW DOOR.**

56. The doctor gives you 5 pills and tells you take one every half hour. How long will they last?

57. Somebody who lives in New York is called American; somebody who lives in London is called British. What do you call somebody who lives at the North Pole?

58. Which is cheaper, to take one friend to the movies twice, or two friends to the movies once?

59. Is it safe to drive a car if you have not slept for seven days?

60. If a man bets you that he can bite his eye, should you take the bet?

61. If he now bets you that he can bite his other eye, should you take the bet?

62. How many balls of string would it take to reach from the Earth to

the Moon?

63. One month, February, has 28 days (except in leap years, when it has 29). Of the remaining months, how many have 30 days?

64. What looks like a horse, moves likes a horse, and is as big as a horse but weighs nothing?

65. How can you travel from Cork to Dublin without passing a single bar?

66. How can you bet a friend he can't take his shoes off by himself and win the bet?

67. How can you make a **cigarette lighter?**

68. What is the capital of Antarctica?

69. What gets higher as it falls?

70. How many queens have been crowned in England since 1820?

71. If you multiply 2 by itself a thousand times, what do you get?

72. How many sides does a circle have?

73. Which is correct to say: "the bigger half" or "the biggest half"?

74. If two is company and three is a crowd, what are four and five?

75. What is E.T. short for?

76. Approximately how many bricks does it take to complete a brick house in England?

77. What do you put on the table, cut, and pass around, but never eat?

78. Why was **King Henry VIII** buried at Windsor Castle?

79. Who went into the lion's den unarmed and came out alive?

80. Tom and Bill are playing in the same **tennis match.** They play four sets and each wins three sets. How is this possible?

81. How can you eat an egg without breaking the shell?

82. *What game begins with a T, has four letters, and is played worldwide?*

83. If these animals all died they would reappear again in a few years. What are they?

84. John has no chickens, nobody gives him eggs, he does not buy eggs, he does not steal eggs, yet he has eggs for breakfast each morning. How?

85. What happens if you light a match in a room completely filled with hydrogen?

86. I have two notes that make $15 but one of them is not a $10 bill. What are they?

87. What department in a hospital is the most dependable?

88. A bright kid is asked by his teacher to multiply together five numbers she will call out. By the time she calls out the third number, he has the correct answer. How come?

89. A boy's bedroom light switch is ten feet from his bed. How can he switch the light off and get into bed before it is dark?

90. What do **reindeer** have that no other animals have?

91. What is the best way of making a **fire** with two sticks?

92. Constantinople is a long word. Can you close the book and spell it?

93. *What five things often come after you?*

94. What kind of rocks are found just below the surface of Lake Superior?

95. *Two Bishops were sitting on a bus together. Which Bishop was wearing the dress?*

96. What is the longest sentence in the English language containing just two words?

97. A trainee secretary is asked to put eight letters in eight envelopes. How likely is it that she will put exactly seven letters in the correct envelopes?

98. Where can you find a triangle with three right angles?

99. How many seconds are there in a year?

100. A woman dropped her watch into a river forty years ago. How could it still be running?

101. If you **fell into the sea,** would you prefer to be nearly drowned or nearly saved?

102. If there are ten apples in a box and you take out six apples, how many apples have you got?

103. In what years do Christmas Day and New Year's Day fall on the same day of the week?

104. Has a horse won the Kentucky Derby six years in a row?

105. What do you get if you cross a brook and a stream?

106. How many **penguins** does the average Eskimo eat in a lifetime?

107. What happened in France on February 29, 1900?

108. If you have an important letter to write is it better to write it on an empty stomach or a full stomach?

109. A brother and sister, born to the same mother and father, have both their birthdays listed on their birth certificates as 12/1/2000, but they were not twins or triplets or part of any other sort of multiple birth. How can this be?

110. What kind of butter will not melt when left out in the sun?

111. In what sport do only the winners move backwards?

112. In what sport do eight ninths of the players move backwards?

113. Why do birds fly south for the winter?

114. If men have two hands and monkeys have four hands then what has just three hands?

115. Where was the first tree planted by human hands in the United States?

116. In what month do Americans eat the least?

117. A male butcher stands 6 feet tall, has a 46-inch chest, and wears size 12 shoes. What would you guess he weighs?

118. What would you call a person who did not have all his fingers on one hand?

119. How do certain individuals have the ability to predict the exact hour of their death?

120. Which is greater, six dozen dozen or half a dozen dozen?

121. What is the best way to

get down from a camel?

122. How could a man be severely injured by being hit by some tomatoes?

123. Why is a giraffe's neck so long?

124. Why do **scuba divers** always fall backward out of a boat into the water?

125. Farmer Jones has three cows and four pigs. If you call a pig a cow, how many cows does Farmer Jones have?

126. What is the hardest thing about

learning to ride a bicycle?

127. What comes after "e" in the alphabet?

128. The number of bacteria in a jar doubles every minute. After one hour the jar is full of bacteria. When was the jar half-full of bacteria?

129. What did Paul Revere say at the end of his epic ride?

130. Would you rather a tiger attack you or a lion?

131. What joins two people but touches only one of them?

132. Otto's car is expensive and reliable but it starts badly most Wednesdays. Why?

133. How do you divide eleven potatoes evenly among four boys?

134. What do Kermit the Frog and Attila the Hun have in common?

135. What has nine legs, two heads, and eats rocks?

136. What do you always get hanging from apple trees?

137. Why are so many famous artists Dutch?

138. How many dollar bills could you fit **between pages** 33 and 34 of a book?

139. When did England begin with an E and end with an E?

140. What animal can jump as high as the Empire State Building?

141. Who was the last man to box Joe Louis?

142. How far can a **dog run into a forest?**

143. If a grandfather clock strikes thirteen, what time is it?

144. Why do some people press elevator buttons with their fingers and others with their thumbs?

145. If there were eight crows on a wall and a farmer shot one, how many would be left?

146. What is the best way to make a sausage roll?

147. Which hand does a nun stir her coffee with?

148. Which triangle has a larger area: one with sides measuring 200, 300, and 400 centimeters, or one with sides measuring 300, 400, and 700 centimeters?

149. Which of the following animals would see best in total darkness: an owl, a leopard, or an eagle?

150. What lies on its back, six feet in the air?

151. Why do so many children have holes in their socks?

152. Which pine has the sharpest needles?

153. How could a man leave a room with two legs and come back with six?

154. What is the best way to make a suit's trousers last?

155. How do you stop a dog barking in the back of a car?

156. If "post" is spelled P-O-S-T and "most" is spelled M-O-S-T, how do you spell the word for what you put in the toaster?

157. What **multiplies by division?**

158. A man throws a ball three feet, it stops and then returns to his hand without touching anything. How come?

159. A Muslim living in England cannot be buried on church ground even if he converts to Christianity. Why not?

160. What word of five letters contains six when two vowels are taken away?

161. How many **bananas** can a grown man eat on an empty stomach?

162. What is the last thing you take off before going to bed at night?

163. How many acorns are there on the average pine tree?

164. If a cat can kill a rat in two minutes, how long would it take a cat to kill a hundred rats?

165. What is white when it is dirty and black when it is clean?

166. It comes with a **motorcycle,** it isn't needed by the motorcycle or the driver, and it's impossible to drive a motorcycle without it. What is it?

167. What can go halfway around the world while never leaving its little corner?

168. What is green, nine feet long, and would injure you very badly if it fell on you out of a tree?

169. In Iran, a Westerner cannot take a photograph of a man with a turban. Why not?

170. A man was an extremely good worker but got the ax on his very first day on the job. Why?

171. What do you call an admiral in the Swiss Navy?

172. Tom's mother had three children. One was called April. One was called May. What was the third one called?

173. Where could you go to see an ancient pyramid, an iceberg, and a huge waterfall?

174. What has four fingers and a thumb but is not a hand?

175. What **cheese** is made backward?

176. If you scratch my back I become virtually useless. What am I?

177. How did an actor get his name up in lights in every theater in the country?

178. You have a tightly corked **bottle of wine.** How can you get the wine out of the bottle without breaking the bottle or taking the cork out of the bottle?

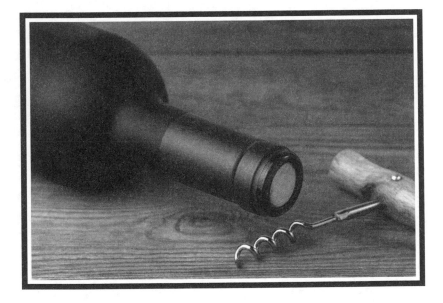

179. How many cells are there in an egg yolk, approximately?

180. What are the chances the first living person you see tomorrow will have more than the average number of arms?

181. What is the easiest way to make a Venetian blind?

182. Where would you find a square ring?

183. Take away my first letter; I remain the same. Now take away my fourth letter; I remain the same. Now take away my last letter; I remain the same. What am I?

184. In China, they hang many criminals, but they will not hang a man with a wooden leg. Why?

185. Why do flamingos stand on one leg?

186. What does a dog do that a man steps into every day?

187. *How do you make a bandstand?*

188. If you stick a **knife in a tree** one foot from the ground and the tree grows one foot every year, how far from the ground will the knife be after twenty years?

189. *In 1961, what were the Poles doing in Russia?*

190. You're standing in line at the ticket desk at an airport. The man in front of you is going to New York. The woman behind you is going to London. Where are you going?

191. A deaf man went into a store to buy a saw. How did he let the storekeeper know he wanted a saw?

192. What was the problem with the wooden car with wooden wheels and a wooden engine?

193. *We all know that two wrongs do not make a right. But what do two Wrights make?*

194. What has eight wheels but can only carry one passenger?

195. *Name three types of car that start with P.*

196. Why was a lady carrying an umbrella on a sunny day?

197. What do people in Scotland call a young white cat?

198. What gets dirty through washing?

199. Write the digits from nine to one backward.

200. An apple tree has six branches. In May, each leaf has fifty branches and grows ten leaves a month. How many leaves will it have in nine months time?

201. I have three heads, nine hands, and thirteen feet. What am I?

202. How can you drop a full glass without spilling any water?

203. How many  **sheep** does it take to make a sweater?

204. What occurs twice in a lifetime, only once in a year, twice in a week, but never in a day?

205. What is the best use for pigskin?

206. What is the best thing to take when you are run down by a car?

207. How do you make a slow horse fast?

208. A **barber** in New York would rather shave two Canadians than one American. Why?

209. What does the world's biggest liner weigh before leaving the dock?

210. Late at night you enter a

dark cabin that

contains a candle, a kerosene lamp, and a wood stove. You have just one match. What do you light first?

211. What mathematical symbol can you put between 5 and 9 to form a number between 5 and 9, using no other digits?

212. What is white, has just one horn, and gives milk?

213. What movie star, who reportedly came close to winning the first Academy Award for Best Actor, was never seen onscreen without a coat?

214. What is orange and sounds like a parrot?

215. How could a man be born in March, have his birthday in May, be born before his father, and marry his mother?

216. What wears shoes but has no feet?

217. How many letters are there in the answer to this question?

218. If you pass the second runner in a race, what position are you now in?

219. *Why did a man get a potato clock?*

220. What should you do if you get a sharp pain in your eye every time you drink a cup of coffee?

221. What can **climb a rope** faster than it can come down a rope?

222. *If a red house is made of red bricks and a blue house is made of blue bricks, what is a greenhouse made of?*

223. Which side of a chicken has the most feathers?

224. What can you put into an empty barrel to make it weigh less?

225. What should you do if your dog chases everyone he sees on a bicycle?

226. What happened to the man who invented the silent **alarm clock?**

227. *What starts with T, ends with T, and is full of tea?*

228. When things go wrong, what can you always count on?

229. How do you know if you are no longer wanted?

230. What did Winston Churchill say to his wife on January 1, 1942?

231. Why do you never see chickens in the zoo?

232. Which is heavier, a pound of feathers or a pound of lead?

233. Okay, let's try that again—which is heavier, a pound of feathers or a pound of gold?

234. Why will over a half a million people be in Washington, D.C., next Christmas?

235. Where are the Kings and Queens of England crowned?

236. Mrs. Jones has five children. Half of them are boys. How can this be?

237. How do you keep a sucker in suspense?

238. What word of just three syllables contains over twenty letters?

239. Why don't U.S. soldiers have rifles any longer?

240. How long will a seven-day grandfather clock run without winding?

241. In round three of a boxing match one of the boxers won by a knockout. Yet not one man had thrown a punch during the whole fight. How come?

242. If it took eight men ten hours to **build a wall,** how long would it take four men to build it?

243. What do you call a man who shaves twenty times a day?

244. You go in through one hole but you come out through three. When you are inside you are ready to go outside but once you are outside you are still inside. What am I talking about?

245. One day, a **skeleton** walked into a bar and ordered a beer. What did he ask for on the side?

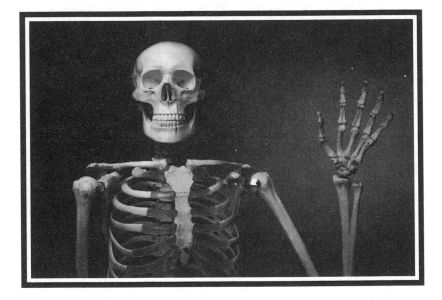

246. A man never worked a day in his life, yet he was named worker of the year. How come?

247. Is the second day of the week pronounced Toozday or Tyewsday?

248. What is the easiest way to join the police?

249. What does it mean when the barometer falls?

250. Three men went into a café and ordered small cups of coffee. Each put an odd number of packets of sugar in his coffee, and altogether they put twenty packets of sugar in their coffee. How could this be?

251. *How many P's in an average pod?*

252. If your boss offers you an 11% increase in salary, followed by an immediate 10% decrease in salary, should you accept the offer?

253. Divide 20 by a half and add 10. What is the result?

254. There were eight ears of corn in a hollow log. Each day a **squirrel** enters the log and leaves with exactly three ears. How many days does it take the squirrel to remove all the ears of corn from the log?

255. What is the name of the island 400 miles east of the North Pole?

256. What do you call a **boomerang** that won't come back?

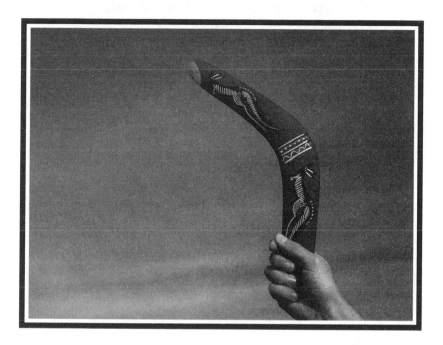

257. When is the best time to buy a canary?

258. If you see a duck paddling downstream in the Nile, where did it come from?

259. Why are elephants such poor dancers?

260. A train sets out from London at noon traveling at 90 miles per hour. Another train sets out from Glasgow at 1 P.M. traveling at 80 miles per hour. Which train is further from London when they meet?

261. Why is it not dangerous to fall off the **edge of a cliff?**

262. What is the difference between theory and practice?

263. If I bought a pet salamander, I would name it Tiny. Why is that a good name?

264. What animal is the most like a tiger?

265. If it takes one man three days to dig two holes, how long will it take him to dig half a hole?

266. *A man is driving toward a railroad crossing at 60 miles an hour, and a train is approaching the same crossing at the same speed. The man and the train are both the same distance from the crossing and neither of them changes speed or changes direction, and the road and the tracks are on the same level. How does the man get across?*

267. What smells the most in a
fish shop?

268. Which travels faster: hot or cold?

269. In a particular town, two out of every
seven people have unlisted telephone
numbers. If there are 14,000 names
in that town's phone book, how many
of those 14,000 people have unlisted
numbers?

270. If the *Mona Lisa* is worth 50 million dollars, how much are two copies of the *Mona Lisa* worth?

271. Which has more tails, one cat or no cat?

272. What vehicle moves inside another moving vehicle, but independently of the outer vehicle and in a different direction?

273. What three letter word completes the first word below and starts the second word?

DON _____ CAR

274. If I gave you ten cents for every quarter you could stand on edge and you stood three quarters on their edge, how much money would you gain?

275. What happens to gold when it is left exposed to the open air for an hour?

276. What has four legs and flies? What else? And what else?

277. An **archaeologist** told her son that she had found a coin on a dig that was dated 200 B.C. He told her it must be a fake, but she insisted it wasn't. Why did he think it was fake, and why didn't the archaeologist?

278. A man works with **numbers** all day, but he's terrible at math. What is his profession?

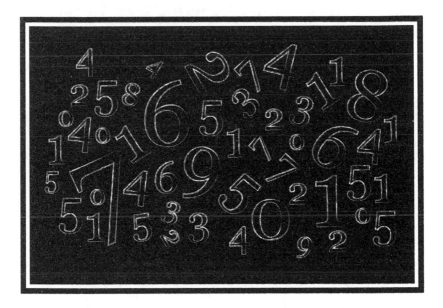

279. Take an eight-letter word, add a letter to it, and it stays the same. What is the word?

280. A woman is standing behind you, and yet you are not standing in front of her. How can this be?

281. The second-closest star to the Earth is Proxima Centauri. What star is nearest the Earth?

282. A mail plane was halfway between Houston and Miami at an altitude of 2,000 feet on a clear, still day. It dropped a 200-pound sack of airmail letters and a 200-pound crash test dummy at the same time. Which hit the ground first?

283. Two field hands are standing in a snow-covered circular field. The taller of the two hands is at the northernmost point of the field, while the shorter hand is standing at the westernmost point. What time is it?

284. What is filled in the morning and emptied at night, except once a year when it is filled at night and emptied in the morning?

285. How can you plant four trees in your garden so that each tree is the same distance from the other three?

286. What can you put **in a cup** that you can't take out?

287. What animal is more sought-after when it is irritated than when it is not?

288. What was the highest mountain in the world before **Mount Everest** was discovered?

289. What do you give the man who has everything?

290. Why is this particular puzzle the last one in the book?

ANSWERS

1. My right elbow.

2. Peacocks do not lay eggs.

3. There is no earth in a hole.

4. There are more of them.

5. Horse racing.

6. Babies.

7. All the doors were locked.

8. In the dictionary.

9. Park in it, man.

10. The same way that short cars should be washed.

11. On the side of her forehead.

12. She is my mother.

13. Your name.

14. Joan is Australian.

15. They are two of a set of triplets.

16. Lunch and dinner.

17. An umbrella.

18. All of them.

19. The score before the game starts is always 0–0.

20. The other end of the rope isn't tied to anything.

21. Two hours after eleven o'clock, when it's one o'clock.

22. A haircut.

23. No, you should spend it.

24. In the ground.

25. Five, since the rope ladder rises with the tide along with the boat.

26. Concrete floors are very difficult to crack!

27. Light it under his nose.

28. Very large hands.

29. No, but it's a good way of finding out who is left.

30. A royal flush requires one ace, and a deck of cards only contains four aces, so these two hands can never arise in the same deal.

31. An old ten-dollar bill is worth ten times as much as a new one-dollar bill.

32. The window.

33. The one in the second bucket, as the water in the first bucket is frozen.

34. Neither—the yolk of an egg is yellow.

35. He drove in reverse.

36. The word "wholesome."

37. The parrot was deaf.

38. At the bottom.

39. Each piece weighs slightly less than one pound, since the sawdust accounts for a small amount of the total weight.

40. The dog walked on her other side.

41. Her father was older than her mother's father.

42. Five minutes.

43. An echo.

44. None; cows can't talk.

45. The president would remain president.

46. No candles burn longer—all candles burn shorter.

47. He had one large haystack.

48. Short.

49. A bed.

50. One hour and twenty minutes is the same amount of time as eighty minutes.

51. The Unfinished Symphony was written by Schubert.

52. The word "wrongly."

53. A hole.

54. The current president wasn't even born yet in 1900!

55. "New door" can be anagrammed to spell "one word."

56. Two hours.

57. Crazy!

58. It's cheaper to take two friends to the movies once—otherwise you have to pay for yourself twice.

59. Yes, if you sleep at night.

60. No; he will take his glass eye out of its socket and bite it.

61. No; he will take out his false teeth and bite his good eye with them.

62. One, if it were big enough.

63. All of them.

64. The shadow of a horse.

65. Go into every one of them.

66. Take your own shoes off at the same time he does.

67. Take the tobacco out.

68. The letter "A."

69. Snow.

70. None—but some princesses have been crowned.

71. Four, every time.

72. Two: the inside and the outside.

73. Neither; two halves are always the same size.

74. Nine.

75. So he can fit in that small spaceship.

76. One. It takes many bricks to build the house, but only one to complete it.

77. A deck of cards.

78. Because he was dead.

79. The lion.

80. They are doubles partners.

81. Get someone else to break the shell.

82. Golf.

83. Mules.

84. He eats duck eggs.

85. Nothing—you need oxygen for an explosion to take place. (So I hope your breathing apparatus doesn't leak!)

86. A $5 bill and a $10 bill. (One is not a $10 bill, and the other one is.)

87. The ultrasound department.

88. The third number is zero.

89. By doing it during the daytime.

90. Baby reindeer.

91. By making sure one of the sticks is a match.

92. I-T.

93. V, W, X, Y, and Z.

94. Wet ones.

95. Mrs. Bishop.

96. "I do."

97. It's impossible. If seven letters all go in the correct envelopes, the eighth letter must also be in the correct envelope.

98. On the surface of a sphere. Imagine traveling from the equator to the North Pole, making a 90° right turn and returning to the equator, then making another 90° right turn to get back to where you started. Draw in those lines, and you've made a triangle with three 90° angles.

99. Twelve. The second of January, the second of February, etc.

100. It's not surprising that the river is still running.

101. It is better to be nearly drowned.

102. You have six apples.

103. They never fall on the same day. The New Year's Day that comes exactly seven days after Christmas Day falls in the next year, and is on a different day of the week than *that* year's Christmas Day.

104. A horse wins the Kentucky Derby every year.

105. Wet feet.

106. None—Eskimos live in the Northern Hemisphere and penguins in the Southern Hemisphere.

107. Nothing—1900 was not a leap year. Every year divisible by 4 is a leap year, except years also divisible by 100 (which aren't leap years), except years also divisible by 400 (which *are* leap years).

108. It's better to write the letter on paper.

109. One was born in the U.K. on January 12, 2000 (where they write dates with the day before the month), while the other was born in the U.S. on December 1, 2000 (where they write dates with the month before the day).

110. A goat!

111. Tug of war.

112. Rowing.

113. Because it's too far to walk.

114. A clock with an hour hand, minute hand, and second hand.

115. In the ground.

116. February—it has fewer days.

117. He weighs meat.

118. Normal. Most people's fingers are evenly distributed between their two hands.

119. The judge tells them.

120. Six dozen dozen is 12 times as many as a half-dozen dozen.

121. You cannot get down from a camel. You get down from a duck.

122. If they were canned tomatoes, they would be very dangerous.

123. Because its head is so far from its body.

124. If they fell forward, they would fall into the boat.

125. Three. Calling a pig a cow doesn't make it a cow.

126. The pavement.

127. The letter "t."

128. It was half-full after 59 minutes.

129. "Whoa!"

130. You would rather the tiger attack the lion.

131. A wedding ring.

132. Otto's car is a BMW (the letters of which begin "badly most Wednesdays").

133. Make mashed potatoes.

134. The same middle name.

135. Nothing. (Did you think the answer was a nine-legged, two-headed rock-eater? Don't be silly—there is no such thing.)

136. Sore arms.

137. They were born in Holland.

138. None. Those two page numbers are on opposite sides of the same sheet of paper.

139. The word "England" has always begun with an E, as has the word "end."

140. Every animal can jump at least as high as the Empire State Building (and almost all of them can jump higher), since the Empire State Building cannot jump.

141. The undertaker.

142. Halfway. After that, it's running out of the forest.

143. Time to get a new clock!

144. To make the elevator move.

145. Just the dead one. The others would fly away.

146. Push it down a hill.

147. Most nuns use spoons.

148. The first triangle is larger. The triangle with sides measuring 300, 400, and 700 centimeters has an area of zero! (The total length of the triangle's two shorter sides equals the length of the longer side, meaning the triangle is actually a line.)

149. In total darkness, none of them could see a thing.

150. A dead ant.

151. So they can put their feet in them.

152. A porcupine.

153. If he leaves the room to get a chair.

154. Make the jacket first.

155. Put him in the front.

156. B-R-E-A-D.

157. An amoeba.

158. He throws it straight up.

159. People who are still alive are not customarily buried anywhere.

160. Sioux.

161. One. After that, his stomach isn't empty any more.

162. Your feet off the floor.

163. None.

164. Faced with 100 rats, the cat would run away!

165. A blackboard.

166. The noise of the motorcycle.

167. A postage stamp.

168. A pool table.

169. It is best to take a photograph of a man with a camera.

170. He was a firefighter.

171. Landlocked Switzerland has no navy. (It does have a civilian merchant marine, though.)

172. Tom.

173. Egypt, Greenland, and Niagara Falls.

174. A glove.

175. Edam, which is "made" backward.

176. A mirror.

177. He changed his name to Exit.

178. Push the cork into the bottle.

179. One.

180. The chances are very high—the average number of arms is just under two (averaging in all the people with one arm or no arms).

181. Poke him in the eyes.

182. At a boxing arena.

183. A postman.

184. They use rope.

185. If they lifted up that leg, they would fall over.

186. Pants.

187. Take away their chairs.

188. One foot. Trees grow from the top, not the bottom.

189. Holding up telegraph wires.

190. If you don't know where you're going, why are you standing in line?

191. He said, "I want a saw."

192. It wooden go!

193. The first airplane.

194. A pair of roller skates.

195. No cars start with pee. Cars start with gasoline.

196. Umbrellas can't walk.

197. A kitten.

198. Bathwater.

199. 1, 2, 3, 4, 5, 6, 7, 8, 9.

200. None; it will be winter.

201. A liar.

202. By filling the glass with milk.

203. Sheep can't knit.

204. The letter E.

205. To keep a pig together.

206. A photo of the license plate.

207. Don't feed him.

208. He makes twice as much money.

209. Anchor.

210. You light the match first.

211. A decimal point, making 5.9.

212. A milk truck.

213. Rin Tin Tin.

214. A carrot.

215. March is the name of the city in which he was born. His birthday was in May, and his father was present at the birth. He became a clergyman, and performed the ceremony when his widowed mother remarried.

216. The pavement.

217. Four. Another possible answer is "0." Yet another possible answer is "23," the number of letters in "the answer to this question." Or, if you answer in another language, you could answer "cinco" (Spanish), "tre" (Italian), and "ni" or "san" (Japanese), among others.

218. Second.

219. Because he had to be at work at nine o'clock.

220. Take the spoon out of the cup.

221. Fire.

222. Glass.

223. The outside.

224. Holes.

225. Take away his bicycle.

226. He won the No-bell Prize.

227. A teapot.

228. Your fingers.

229. When they take down your photograph at the police station.

230. "Happy New Year."

231. They cannot afford the price of admission.

232. They both weigh the same.

233. A pound of feathers weighs 16 ounces, while a pound of gold only weighs 12 ounces, so the pound of feathers weighs more. This is because feathers are weighed using the avoirdupois scale, whereas gold is measured using the troy scale.

234. They live there.

235. On the head.

236. All of them are boys.

238. Alphabet.

239. The rifles are long enough already.

240. Without winding, it won't run at all.

241. The boxers were both women.

242. No time at all; the first eight men have already built it.

243. A barber.

244. Putting on a sweater.

245. A mop.

246. He was a night watchman.

247. Neither; it is pronounced "Monday."

248. With handcuffs.

249. The nail has come out of the wall.

250. The first two men used one packet of sugar each. The third man used eighteen packets, which is a very odd number of sugar packets to put in a small coffee.

251. One.

252. No. You start out earning 100% of your current salary. Increase that by 11% and you're up to 111%. Decrease that by 10% and you're down to 99.9%, so if you accept this deal, your salary will end up going down slightly.

253. Fifty. Dividing by a half is the same as multiplying by two.

254. Eight days. Each day he leaves the stump with one ear of corn and two squirrel ears.

255. There is no such island. Everywhere on Earth is south of the North Pole.

256. A stick.

257. When it's going cheap!

258. An egg.

259. Because they have two left feet.

260. This is a fairly well-known trick question, and if you know the trick, you may have answered that when the trains meet, they are each the same distance from London. But this is not really the case. It is true that the front ends of the trains are the same distance from London when they meet. But trains are long, and the back end of the train from Glasgow is further from London than any part of the train from London, so the correct answer is the train from Glasgow.

261. Falling is not the problem—it's hitting all the rocks at the bottom that's the problem.

262. In theory there is no difference between theory and practice, but in practice there is.

263. Because it would be my newt.

264. Another tiger.

265. There's no such thing as half a hole.

266. His surviving relatives buy one (a cross, that is) for his grave.

267. The shopowner's nose.

268. Hot, because you can catch cold.

269. None of them.

270. The copies are worthless, since they are both forgeries.

271. No cat, because one cat has one tail, but no cat has nine tails.

272. An elevator inside an ocean liner.

273. "Key" completes the word "donkey," and a key starts a car.

274. You would lose 45 cents, since I would be giving you 10 cents in exchange for each one.

275. Someone tries to steal it.

276. Two birds, or a dead horse, or two pairs of pants.

277. The son assumes that the coin is engraved with a date of 200 B.C., which would mean the coin must be fake, since people who were alive in 200 B.C. did not use "B.C." (The term "B.C." was first proposed in the 6th century A.D.) In fact, though, the coin had no date engraved on it, but was found wrapped in a cloth pouch, which was carbon-dated 200 B.C.

278. He's an anesthesiologist.

279. Envelope.

280. You and she are standing back to back.

281. The sun.

282. Neither. The plane was over the Gulf of Mexico so they both hit water.

283. Wintertime.

284. A stocking.

285. Plant three at the corners of an equilateral triangle. Then make a mound of dirt in the center of the triangle so that its highest point is the top vertex of a regular tetrahedron whose base is the triangle, and plant the fourth tree at the top of the mound.

286. A crack.

287. An oyster, which produces a pearl when it is irritated by a grain of sand.

288. Mount Everest.

289. Antibiotics.

290. Because there aren't any more after it.

About the Authors

Paul Sloane lives in England. He writes and speaks on innovation and lateral thinking in business. He studied engineering at Cambridge University. He and his wife have three daughters and five grandchildren, all of whom get the lateral puzzles treatment. He hosts the Lateral Puzzles Forum at www.lateralpuzzles.com.

Des MacHale lives in Ireland and is Emeritus Professor of Mathematics at University College Cork where he taught for 40 years. He is interested in puzzles of all sorts, particularly ones that show the fun side of mathematics and logic. He and his wife, Anne, have five children who currently live in Sweden, Switzerland, the United States, and Ireland. He is also interested in music, words, jokes, geology, and John Ford's movie *The Quiet Man*. He has written over 60 books on various subjects, with about a dozen more in the pipeline.